The sun will rise soon and Bella will wake up . . .

For Hannah H, Tani K, Luka and Nicholas.

Special thanks to: Margaret Connolly, Sue Flockhart,
Erica Wagner and Trish Hayes.

Bella's BAD HAIR DAY

Stephen Michael King

Cock-a-doodle-doo

ALLEN & UNWIN
SYDNEY · MELBOURNE · AUCKLAND · LONDON

But Bella's mum was already being pestered by unpredictable pets.

She had no time to listen to Bella's horrible hair problems.

Bella's dad was calmly playing
Beethoven's 'Ode to Joy'
on his baby grand piano
and didn't notice anything
but the sound of his music.

Didn't anyone realise it was going to be a horrible, horrific, horrendous hair day?

'Bellissimo,' said Sam the hairdresser as he kissed the air. 'I shall **cut** everything **off** except for this little **curl**.'

Bella escaped before the first SNIP.

If it had been Christmas,
Bella might have been able
to decorate her hair with
twinkly tinsel,
bouncy baubles
and a golden star . . .

and have everyone
believe she was a
Christmas tree . . .

that had been **hit** by a **cyclone!**

Bella remembered the days,
not so long ago, even as close
as yesterday, when her hair
was as soft and flowing as
her summer dress,

and as shiny as a shampoo
commercial.

Ahhh, life was blissful back then,
thought Bella . . .

until she was rudely
interrupted by Reginald
the carpenter's bear.

'I can flatten it, if you like,'
said Reginald.

Bella did **NOT** like!

Then **Urrgh** and his
woolly mammoth appeared.

'Your hair looks very
becoming today,'
said Urrgh.

'gggghhhh!'

groaned Bella.

What
was she to do?

If only a superhero could whisk her away.

If only
bad hair was
nouveau trendo
at the moment . . .

If only . . .   if only she had a hat!

A tall hat,   a fat hat,

a hat that could hide all her
messed, mashed and muddled-up hair.

Anything would do.

Well . . .

as long as it was stylish.

Unfortunately for Bella . . .

windy days

just love

hats . . .

and lost sea birds.

One particular
lost sea bird
liked the look of Bella.

So she landed on top
of Bella's horrible, horrific,
horrendeous hair . . .

and left a little lost egg.

Bella ran home to her mother.
'Don't worry, Bella,' said her mum.
'At least a **flying rhinoceros** didn't land **in it.**'

Mum

brushed,

swished

and twirled Bella's hair
into what Dad called
'a breathtakingly, beautiful bouffant'.

'Ahhhhhh,' sighed Bella.

'Now **today** is perfect.'

First published in 2013

Allen & Unwin
83 Alexander Street
Crows Nest NSW 2065
Australia
Phone: (61 2) 8425 0100
Email: info@allenandunwin.com
Web: www.allenandunwin.com

A Cataloguing-in-Publication entry is available
from the National Library of Australia
www.trove.nla.gov.au

ISBN 978 174331 361 9

Cover and text design by STINGart
Set in Skizzors and SpillMilk by STINGart

Stephen Michael King created these illustrations
using pen, brush and black ink. Art was coloured
and compiled using InDesign and Photoshop.

This book was printed in April 2013
by C & C Offset Printing Co. Ltd,
C & C Building, Chunhu Industrial Estate,
Pinghu, Longgang, Shenzhen, Guangdong, PRC, 518111

1 3 5 7 9 10 8 6 4 2

smkbooks.com